THE ARRANGEMENT

Vol. 11

H.M. Ward

www.SexyAwesomeBooks.com

Laree Bailey Press

COPYRIGHT

Laree Bailey Press
First Edition: Oct 2013

THE ARRANGEMENT

Vol. 11

CHAPTER 1

The moment seems unreal. Never in a million years did I think that I would ever see Sean Ferro on his knee in front of me. The idea of him proposing is preposterous, and yet, here he is on one knee holding up a ring. My legs feel like they're going to give way, but I don't move. It's one of those few moments in life where time slows to a crawl, and I'm acutely aware of everything around me. The scent of the ocean, the sound of the waves, and the fuzzy new sweats are caressing my skin. The fireplace crackles and a log breaks, sending a spray of sparks up the chimney. I can't smile or speak. I'm suspended somewhere between reality and a dream. There's nothing that could break this moment. I want it to last forever; I want to treasure it as one of the few times that Sean's let me into his heart.

Normally this man is so closed down, and so guarded, that it's impossible to know what he's thinking. Most days I haven't a clue of how he feels or what he actually wants. I think I can see his affection for me in his eyes, but it's not the same as hearing the words fall from those beautiful lips. I crave to know what he thinks more than anything else, because those little confessions form an intimate connection between us.

There have been a few times where Sean seemed unguarded—Cardiac Hill in the snow and this morning on the beach—but they've been fleeting. That version of Sean appears in short bursts and is a glory to behold, and I crave more. I live for those moments, and now that I'm in one I'm so afraid of shattering it.

In the past, Sean has tried to open up, but then he did a one-eighty. That was more crushing than if he'd never let me get close to him at all. The thing is, I can't blame him. I'm not saying it doesn't make me want to throw things and my eye twitch—because it does—but I understand his hesitation.

I know what it means to try and love again after living through such a devastating loss. There was a time when I thought that I could simply shut everyone out. Love isn't a requirement to live, and I'd planned to do without. It made sense at the time. Loss was too gruesome to bear, but then I met Sean and I knew there was something about him. Our fates intertwined, and it's finally more than that. He wants me and he's going to say as much. That ring sparkles in front of me like a promise I thought he'd never say.

I suck in a shaky breath and finally manage to tear my gaze away from the ring and over to Sean's face. He looks vulnerable, with a childlike expression. The hardened mask he constantly wears is gone, and I only see sincerity mingling with hope in those blue eyes. It kills me that he's been so alone for so long. It's like he doesn't trust another soul on earth, but in this moment, he trusts me. There was a time that I thought Sean didn't have any hope, and that was what made us different from one another. However, the emotion is clear. Hope. It's plainly visible, unmasked and unguarded. Sean thinks I can save him, and that he can save me. He thinks we have a future together.

Too many thoughts rush through my mind and spiral into a pit of concern. What about that darkness within him? Where did it go? Does being Sean's wife mean that he needs that sexual control over me, that he'll twist and manipulate my fears to suit his needs? I know he says that part of him is gone, but it can't be, can it? It's been there too long to simply vanish. I'm not foolish enough to think that we'll have a happily ever after, not with the amount of heartache we've had. But maybe we can make it to a bright spot in our otherwise hellish lives.

Can we really save each other?

The concerns turn to whispers and blur together. I can no longer identify which worries are valid and which are fear. Anxiety trickles down my spine in a cold sheet as

Sean licks his lips. His mouth parts and his voice pours out soft and unsure. "Avery Stanz, would you consider taking this ring and—"

Every inch of my skin is tingling like my life is about to radically transform. *Don't smile, don't do it.* For all I know he's going to ask me something stupid and I need to keep my wits about me so I can kick him.

But, oh God, I want to grin and clasp my hands together. Sean wouldn't pretend to propose and then not do it. There's a happy dance building inside of me, making my heart flutter and the corners of my lips tip up. Anticipation and excitement are coursing through my veins as the words come from his heart.

Everything is about to change.

Then, it does. The door to the little beach shack slams open and hits the concrete wall hard. The sound cuts off Sean's question and he jumps to his feet when he sees who's standing there.

CHAPTER 2

Gabe. The man is covered in sweat like he's been running. He walks quickly toward us, straightening his rumpled suit. "I wasn't here and I didn't see this," his hands fly in the air like he wants to punch something, "whatever the fuck this is. Avery, you know better. I told you." Worry pinches his brow as he lets out a rush of air and points at the door. "Go, get out of here and for the love of God, don't wear the fucking bracelet when you're not working. If Black asks, I didn't find you. You were already gone."

For a moment all I can do is blink, "But, why are you—'

Gabe looks at Sean and some unspoken message passes from one man to the other. Gabe repeats, "Go. Separate. Find Mel and work out your timeline before you check in tonight."

But I don't move. "Gabe, what's happening?" What's wrong? Because something is very off.

The old man stares at me and for a moment I think he's seeing someone else, maybe a daughter. I remind him of someone he cared about, someone that he failed somehow. The haunted expression lingers at the back of his eyes as if he's seeing a ghost. "Avery, Black knows about you two. She's always known, but she tolerated it. Something changed today. I don't know what, but her orders were to find you and remind you that you are her property, and to use excessive force in doing so."

Sean tries to pull me away from Gabe, but I know the old guy won't hurt us. Besides, if he was here to take my head off, he would have done it already. "Sean, it's all right. He's warning us, and I bet that he's risking a lot to do it."

Gabe's eyes remain locked on mine. His voice is pleading. "Something changed. I know you won't run, but you need to get away from her. Quit and walk away before this gets worse. Someone's going to end up in a body bag before this is over and I sure as hell don't want it to be you."

Without another word, Sean pulls at my hand and gives me the keys to his car. "Go back to the dorm and lock yourself in your room. I'll check on you to make sure you're all right."

"Sean?" I don't like this. Gabe and Sean exchange looks, like there's more to be said but they don't want to say it in front of me. It feels like I was booted off of cloud nine, did a free fall, and landed smack on my face. Emotional whiplash is a bitch. "What else is going on? You know that Black knew about us, didn't you? Then why is she—"

"No, we're not discussing this right now." Sean's gaze slips over me quickly. "Where's the bracelet?"

"At the bottom of my purse. I didn't realize…" I didn't think she'd be tracking me for kicks. It's the first time that I really realize Miss Black isn't the business woman she appears to be. I've been thinking of her as a boss, but she isn't. She's more than that, much more. My jaw flops around. There are so many things I want to say, but they all sound stupid now. I'm naïve. Miss Black isn't some passive woman trying to make a quick buck. Call girls are her empire and she's the queen, which makes me a pawn.

Sean watches me for a second and I get the feeling that the imaginary marriage is slipping between my fingers. "Avery, we'll fix this. We need to proceed like nothing's wrong, like we don't know. You didn't see Gabe, and we weren't together today. Go into her office tonight and act like you don't care. Do whatever you have to do to get in and out of there quickly. If I thought she'd hurt you, there's no way I'd send you in, but Black has other plans." He glances at Gabe. "What'd she want you to do if you found us together?"

"Throw punches and snap a few bones, enough to make her point but not so much that she needs major medical attention."

Gabe stops speaking suddenly. There's more there, something he's not telling us.

Sean nods and takes my shoulders in his hands and looks into my eyes. "Listen, everything will be fine. I'll make certain of it. I'll grab Pete and Jon if I have to. God knows they owe me one. I'll get you away from her. You'll show up later and this will be the last night you work for that woman." There's a faint smile on his lips as he leans in close enough to kiss me and whispers, "After tonight, you'll be mine, and I very much hope that you'll say yes." He smiles at me, kisses my forehead, and pushes me toward the door.

CHAPTER 3

That's the end of the conversation. I'm shoved in the car and am back on the road before I can think. Driving past the sand dunes, I wonder about Black's other thug and what to do if that guy finds me. God, I feel sick. It's like someone has been playing PONG with my stomach. I crack the window and creep along the road until I hit the parkway.

It feels like I'm missing something that should be obvious, but I don't see it. When I started working for Black, Mel told me that I could leave—that I could take one client and be done with it—but things didn't work out that way. It's like I'm her only call girl. For a second, I wonder how many women Black employs. I've only ever seen Mel, but that doesn't mean there aren't other girls. I've seen the thick files on her desk, right before she enters the data into her computer. Black's operation takes in a lot of money, and she has a shortage of girls.

Even so, something doesn't sit right. I can't put my finger on what's wrong, but it feels perilous. Is there another connection between all these people? Gabe, Black, Naked Guy, Mel, Henry Thomas, and Sean Ferro. I think back, trying to make connections between them. But, other than Henry and Sean, there aren't any obvious ones.

Maybe I'm a paranoid psycho for even thinking this way, but it feels like I'm standing in the middle of a chessboard and all the other players are moving into position. My gut instinct is that it has nothing to do with being a call girl, but that doesn't make any sense. All these people are in my life because I'm a hooker. There's no real connection between these people. Well, that's not entirely true. There is one connection between all of them—me.

My throat tightens. Am I being played? If so, why? I mean, I'm a nobody. If my name showed up in the paper, accused of some heinous crime, no one would care. And, my sexting files? Being outed as a hooker would end my career, but it would also get Black's ass thrown into prison. It would ruin both of us. So, why would she do that? That can't be it. Black is trying to keep a hold on me, and maybe it's about the money and nothing more.

I try to shove the puzzle pieces together over and over again, but they don't fit. I'm the only link between all these people and I'm also the only person getting dicked around. No one messes with Black or Gabe or Thug #2. Damn it! What the hell is that guy's name? I need to remember.

When I get back to the dorm, I park at the back of the lot and run to the building and up the staircase. By the time I'm on my floor, I'm sweating and shaking. Heart pounding, I race to Mel's room and knock.

She's always here a few hours before a client, getting ready, but she doesn't answer.

Instead Asia pops her head out. "What's up, Avery?" She looks me over and arches an eyebrow. "Were you making-out with seaweed again?"

Again? WTF? Ignoring her jab, I ask, "Where's Mel?"

Asia throws out her hip and rests her head against the edge of the door. "Working. Her boss called her in early. She said that she'd meet you there."

The skin on the back of my neck prickles instantly and spreads, covering my arms and snaking around my neck like a noose. I stand shivering and speechless.

Asia looks back into the darkened room. It's pitch black and a voice I don't recognize calls her name. She says, "One second," over her shoulder and then steps out into the hallway, pulling the door closed behind her. "What's the matter? You look like you're going to hurl. Is Mel all right?"

I nod a few times and force a smile. It feels like a trap. There are neon signs lighting up and exploding in my head, but I still can't see the connection. Hiding my apprehension, I manage a normal tone and make something up. "Yeah, everything's great. I just thought we were riding to work together, that's all. No biggie."

Asia knows I'm lying but doesn't say anything. She has the look on her face that my mother used to have when I told a bald-faced lie. Asia tucks her hair behind her ear. "Call me if you need anything, or if Mel does. I'm around tonight." She winks at me and tips her head toward the door, indicating that they're not knitting in there.

"Will do!" My voice is too chipper. I'm a horrible liar.

CHAPTER 4

I walk down the hallway to my room and slide the key into the lock. I'd rather smack my skull against the door, but that won't fix anything. The idea that someone is playing me makes me irate. I didn't think I was that stupid. Kicking the door open, I go inside and toss my keys on the table as the door swings shut behind me. It's dark, except for Amber's pink lava lamp glowing dimly next to her bed. Amber must be out at dinner or something.

A sound catches my ear, something like a foot sliding across the carpet. My skin prickles like I'm not alone. The sound was as light as a cat's paw, barely there, but I heard it. Turning quickly, I grope the wall, looking for the light switch. My thumb catches the edge, so I shove it upward. Light pours from the ceiling as my eyes dart through the shadows scanning for a sign of what made the sound. My muscles are flexed, like I'm ready to run or beat the shit out of someone. God, if Amber is hiding in her closet, I'm going to lose it.

My gaze flicks to a pair of scissors on the counter. I pluck them from their place and hold them like a dagger, stalking slowly toward the source of the noise. It came from Amber's side of the room. I feel stupid, because I'm certain that no one is there. It was probably a card falling to the floor or something dumb, because I don't hear anything else. It's quiet, save for the sound of my breathing.

Stepping slowly toward her closet, I reach for the knob, and jerk it open. Jumping back, I hold tighter to the shears and raise them up over my head, expecting to need to stab something, but nothing is there. Just clothes. There are no nefarious feet hidden behind Amber's dresses and no glowing red eyes.

I stumble back and let out a rush of air as a shiver works its way up my arm. I sit down hard on Amber's bed and try to calm down. My heart is racing like crazy and I can barely breathe. What the hell was I going to do with a pair of scissors anyway? I don't think I'd have the guts to stab someone in the face if it came down to it.

Those are situations I'd rather not think about, because part of me thinks I'm so far gone that I'd do whatever I had to do. Pretending I'm still human, that I could use my deductive reasoning to outsmart someone, rather than stab them to death, sounds better. As if I'd be mentally superior to anyone. I'm shaking, trying to shoo away the worries that swarm around me.

What if…? What if…? They whisper the words at me over and over again.

What if nothing! No one is here. I don't have to think about what I can do or what I would do. No one is stalking me and my imagination is in hyperdrive. I just need to slow down.

I go for my phone and for the first time ever, I think about texting Sean. I want to tell him that I'm freaked and hear his voice, but I know I shouldn't. If Black saw it, she'd have proof that we were together. But if she already knows, maybe I have nothing to lose? I'm close to trembling and turning into a snotty mess. But then I see Gabe's face and hear his voice in my mind, and I can't give Black more ammo to shoot me with. I can't text Sean unless someone is actually killing me.

It takes me a moment to get my hysterical self under control and punch in a different number. Mel picks up on the third ring. "Can't talk now, Avery." Her voice is clipped, but it doesn't sound like she's shoved under someone's floorboards or getting her neck slit. What the hell is wrong with me? Mel can handle herself. I'm the question mark, not her.

I spit it out, "I'm quitting. I can't take this anymore, Mel. I'm not coming."

"You better. I'll come over there and haul your ass from that dorm room. Some jackass booked a threesome and guess whose names got pulled. I'm relieved it's you and not Trish this time—"

Crap, she doesn't know that Sean's the guy who hired us. I don't have time to explain that right now. "Mel, shut up and listen. Something weird is going on. I'm majorly creeped out. I swear to God that it feels like someone's been in my room."

She shushes someone and there's a moment filled with the sound of her hand over the phone. "Look around while I'm on the phone. Hurry up."

"I already did. No one's here. Nothing's out of place, but it feels wrong." I bite the tip of my finger and glance at the door again to make sure it's still locked.

"You're just worked up. Don't worry about anything. Go change in my room if you want." I know she's just saying it to be nice, but we're both thinking the same thing. Someone was in here.

Glancing around again, I try to pinpoint what's been touched, but nothing is obvious. After switching my phone to the other ear, I tell her, "Asia is doing someone in your room."

Mel laughs. "Good for her. It took them long enough. Damn." Her hand covers the phone again before she adds, "I gotta go, chica. I'll see you at Black's in a bit." The line goes dead.

I toss my phone onto my bed and walk into the bathroom. My heart has resumed a normal pace and I'm starting to feel stupid for being so freaked out. The first time I stayed home alone I was 9 years old and I couldn't calm down the entire time. Every noise was a threat. I finally grabbed our fat tabby cat and bunkered down at the top of the staircase with my little heart beating uber fast. I totally thought I was going to die. The cat on the other hand thought I was insane because I wouldn't let him leave my side, but he didn't know about my cat-in-the-face attack plan. It would have worked, too. A startled, orange, thirty-pound cat smacking into some dude's head would have thrown him off balance long enough for me to jump out the bedroom window. Maybe I have too much imagination, but when I get freaked out, I can get a little bit weird. Like now.

Leaning into the shower stall, I turn on the water. After letting it flow over my hand for a few seconds, I adjust the temperature. Pulling off my shoes, I toss them on the floor and pad over to the closet to get my bathrobe, my little basket filled with soaps and hair care products, and the best razor in the world. Amber's not here. This is nice. There's no sign of Naked Guy and I can take my time. Sean and Gabe are looking out for me. There's nothing to worry about, although I may need to consider the purchase of a new attack cat. Amber wouldn't notice.

God, my life is a mess. Graduation can't come fast enough. I'll get my degree and finally get things rolling. I can picture myself there, in graduate school, and how my life will look after I make it through my degree. I think about those things, about the future that seems to be constantly crumbling as I slip out of my clothes and pull on my robe. My mood is turning to crap. I need to sniff the entire bottle of honeysuckle soap. Maybe mix it up with sweet pea and warm vanilla sugar. I'll smell like a yummy fruit cocktail. They totally need to make cake scented body wash. I'd probably eat the bottle. Mmmm. Cake. Sighing, I set the basket of goodies on the ledge inside the stall, before pulling the door shut. The little room is like the inside of a cloud as steamy mist billows from the shower stall.

My gaze finally lifts to the mirror. Every thought falls out of my head as panic comes back, full force, choking me. Steam swirls in the humid air, fogging the glass, as letters slowly appear.

BE AFRAID

CHAPTER 5

I watch without blinking as words form in front of my eyes. For half a second I wonder if Amber is screwing with me, but there's no way. She wouldn't have written this. The edges of the letters start to drip down the glass. My body tenses as my arms start to shake. Before I can think, I react. My hand wipes away the words and condensation smears across the glass. Rivulets drip from the mirror and moisture clings to my hand.

I stand there, frozen for a second, and then bust out of the bathroom and run down the hallway. I bang on Asia's door like a lunatic and I honestly have no idea what I'm going to say, because everything sounds nuts.

Asia peeks through the crack in the door. Her face is flushed and her hair is messy. "You have really bad timing."

"This is going to sound crazy, but can you guys come down to my room?"

Asia gives me a really weird look and nearly closes the door in my face. I manage to get my fingers into the space between the door and the jamb before she closes it. "Ahhh! I didn't mean it like that."

She opens the door a little bit and looks really annoyed. "Talk fast, Avery."

"Someone is messing with me and they only seem to do it when I'm alone. I need to get ready for work and my roommate is gone. Can you guys come and hang out in my room? You can stay there for the rest of the night."

"We were going to stay here for the rest of the night."

"Yeah, but Mel will be back around two o'clock. I'll give you my room until morning." I give her my best puppy dog face and clutch my hands together under my chin. Begging looks awesome on me.

Her eyes flick up and down like she's considering it. "What about your roommate?"

"She's fine with it." Mainly, because she doesn't know about it, but hey, Amber's locked me out enough times and this is totally worth it. Dropping my hands, I straighten. "Please, Asia. I'll only be there for half an hour and then the place is yours."

She rolls her eyes and looks back at the bed. "Wait." Asia pushes the door shut and I hear her muffled voice through the wall. A moment later she reappears wearing a bathrobe, with a tall guy behind her. He takes her hand and leans in, pressing kisses to her neck. Apparently no bed isn't a problem for him, because he keeps kissing her like they're still alone. His hands slip around her waist from behind and cup her breasts over her robe. Asia moans as she tips her head to the side, before replying, "Deal. You're homeless until 10am."

"Done." Holy shit, this is awkward. They're much more into public displays of affection than I am. The way they behave makes my face turn red. The guy does whatever he wants and Asia lets him. It doesn't matter that they're in the middle of the hall.

I race back to my room. The shower is still running. I duck inside before I see much more and get dressed as fast as possible.

The sounds of sex reach me through the walls as I pull on my lingerie and stockings. Miss Black is still going to check everything even though Mel and I aren't actually having a three way. After applying my make-up, I grab my purse and duck out the door, but not before seeing Mel's sweet, meek roommate doing insanely kinky things. I need to scrub my brain with bleach. I'm a hooker and what I just saw Asia doing shocked me.

You're a bad hooker, a little voice tells me.

Yeah, that's my problem.

Oh crap, now I'm having conversations with myself. I growl as I race down the stairs with my sneakers on my feet and my fuck-me heels in hand. After finding my car, I drive to Black's as quickly as possible. I don't want to be alone and I'm so spooked that I'd rather be around her than no one at all.

When I step out of the elevator, Gabe is there. He doesn't look at me, but he falls in step and says in a low voice, "I've got your back. Ferro will rip this place apart looking for you if we aren't on time tonight, so don't linger, and Avery," I look over at him and swallow hard. "Don't piss her off. She's in a mood and if I didn't know better, I'd think someone's got her by the balls." Gabe suddenly veers off down a different hall without further explanation of anything.

I make my way to Miss Black's office and can hear her talking to someone on the phone. Her voice carries through the door. "I'm well aware of that and you can rest assured that it won't happen. I know what I'm doing. Yes, well—" her voice cuts off abruptly. Gabe must have told her I was here, either that or she can see through wood.

When I step up to her door, I find it's opened a crack. I look inside without pushing the door open.

"Stop lurking, Avery. It's rude." Miss Black stands and walks over to me. She's dressed neatly and looks completely respectable. You'd never know that she made her living selling sex. She snaps her fingers at me. "I don't like that dress, so I hope you have something better underneath."

I know better than to say anything. The little black dress is pretty with a scoop neck and a swishy skirt. It doesn't scream hooker. Apparently we can't both look respectable. Black narrows her gaze and shoots me a disgusted look, followed by an overdramatic sigh. Wonderful. She's even worse than Gabe let on.

I hate this, but I do it anyway. Reaching around to the side, I unzip my dress, and step out of it. I'm wearing a black lacy demi bra with bits of purple trim along the cups. I'm practically spilling out the top. The bottoms are a black cheeky panty with a bow right above my bare ass. It's been tickling me every time I take a step and since scratching my ass is a fashion *faux pas*, it's been driving me nuts.

"Turn," Black commands with her hand on her chin and a look of sheer annoyance on her face. She lets out an irritated breath when she sees my back. "What is this?" She reaches for the bow and tugs it, nearly knocking me over. "I told you to only wear string bottoms. These aren't good enough. No one cares about your bow covered butt, Avery."

Miss Black walks to her desk and opens a drawer. When she comes back, she doesn't even look at me. Instead, she takes scissors and clips twice. The piece of fabric that made up my cute little panties falls to the floor. I want to cover myself and yell at her, but I don't.

I remain rigid and stare straight ahead, chanting to myself, *Shut up, Avery. Don't say a word. Don't fight back. Just stare straight ahead.* It's my theme song, or I swear to God, I'd hit her.

CHAPTER 6

I'm so bent out of shape and such an emotional mess that I could totally go all ninja on her ass. The thing is, I think Black would kill me and stuff my head in her stapler drawer before I could throw a punch. Actually having mad skills isn't anything like the cartoonish self-defensive stuff I know, which is comprised of two things: falling to the floor and screaming. Crap like that doesn't help when your boss cuts off your underwear in the middle of her office.

Black walks over to her closet and pulls out a dark garment bag. She glances up at me. "I'm taking this out of your check." She holds it out for me. I step towards her like it's totally normal to walk around in heels, thigh highs, and a bra. It doesn't matter that my snatch patch isn't covered. At least it shouldn't, not by now, not if I was doing what I was supposed to be doing, but since the only client I've been with is Sean, it still bothers me.

"Stop sulking and put it on." She snaps at me again, before sitting on the edge of her desk and folding her arms across her chest.

I take the dress out of the bag and manage to bite my tongue. There's nothing to it. I pull the clothing off the hanger and slip it on. Apparently I'm taking too long, because Miss Black huffs over and slaps my hands. "Let me do it. Honestly, Avery, I have no idea how you can be so utterly incompetent and so desirable at the same time. It seems like everyone is asking for you lately. I've had a hard time selling anyone in your place."

She yanks on my girls, making my eyes bug out of my head, shifting them under the dress. She's horrible. I hope she gets hit by a truck later. I try to focus on what she said instead of what she's doing to the girls. "In my place? Why, did someone try to book me tonight, besides Mr. Ferro?"

Miss Black runs her hand along my bra and smooths the fabric. The neckline dips, forming a thin V as it comes across my chest and down to my waist. This is a slut dress. It's skin tight, too short, and backless.

Her gaze flicks up to mine. "Of course. Every client you've had wanted you, plus some. Your reputation is spreading, which is wonderful. They all want you. I've received several calls from clients—new and old— who want to book you at the same time. It's a full moon or something. I got the rest to accept someone else, but one man insisted on having you and paid for it. I couldn't tell him no."

"You double booked me?" I sound appalled.

Miss Black answers without looking at my face. Her eyes rove my body, looking at the new dress. "It's not a big deal, just go by the second room before you leave the city. He said he'd wait for you. I explained that you had a previous obligation."

My jaw is clicking and I'm pretty sure my head is ready to spin off my shoulders. "Miss Black, I actually wanted to talk to you." My boss looks up and I know that I have her full attention. Don't be timid, Avery. Spit it out. Squaring my shoulders, I say, "I don't think I can do this anymore. I mean, if tonight wasn't with Mel, I don't know what I would have done."

She spins me around and pulls the dress into place at my shoulders and smooths more of the fabric as she runs her palms over my hips, before swatting my butt. "I told you to lose weight. This is becoming a problem."

Did she just say that I'm fat? Blinking, I shake my head and stare at her. "Did you hear me? I don't want to do this anymore."

Miss Black steps away from my back and walks around to face me. There's a pleasant smile on her face, very similar to the one she had when I first met her. "Avery, dear, do you know how much money you'll make if we continue to book each of these men once a week—once a month, even? Your weekly pay check will be well into dreamland territory and all you have to do is keep these rich men begging for more. I have no idea how you do it, but they clearly want you." She folds her arms over her chest while she stares at my cleavage. She pokes at my left boob, like it's not in the right place.

What just happened? I quit twice and she basically ignored me. "Miss Black—"

Before I can say another word, she steps toward me, close enough to kiss, and presses her finger to my lips. Her voice is a lethal whisper. "If I only knew how you did it, I could show each one of my girls and there'd be more money than any of us ever dreamed, more money than you'd make in a lifetime, Avery. There's something about you that makes these men crave you and willing to pay any price to have you sate their lust, but somehow you always leave them wanting more. And they want so much more..." Her dark eyes are on my mouth and the moment has moved from weird to utterly uncomfortable. Miss Black's perfect ruby red lips pull into a smile as her finger slips away.

I stand there frozen, wondering what she means by that. Her long dark lashes are lowered and she remains too close for too long, breathing deeply with her lips parted like she wants to say something else.

The sound of static saves me. Black rolls her eyes and turns back toward her desk. "Mel is here." Gabe's voice through the intercom is detached and devoid of emotion.

What? Mel was supposed to be here already. What the hell is Gabe talking about?

A moment later, Mel is at the door. "Hey, Miss Black." She bounds into the room with a fake smile to hide her nerves. Mel isn't afraid of anyone, but she's fearful of Black. Mel's wearing a flirty red dress similar to the one I had on before my shameful scolding. She spins and it floats up in a circle, showing off her lacy thigh highs and new panties. "What do you think?"

"It's perfect, Mel."

My jaw drops and I make a face. "What! That's just like the dress I had on!"

"Yes, dear, but Mel wearing a cute dress is ironic, while on you, it's just cute and cute doesn't sell."

Mel looks over at me and whistles. "Hot damn, Avery. That dress is tight. I like how the little bits of purple lace peak out from your bra. That is one hot look."

I want to strangle her. Miss Black smiles. "It appears that one of Avery's talents is teasing, so she should play up the anticipation, don't you think?"

"Fuck, yeah. I'd do you looking like that." Mel laughs with Black as they both head over to the table outside her office. The conversation continues, but the words Sean said come back to me. He thinks she has a thing for me, but I don't get that vibe from her. Mel teases, that's all. She wasn't serious.

"So, who are we doing?" Mel asks, as Black measures her. She isn't asked to strip. I guess the hands on treatment is just for me. WTH?

"Mr. Ferro." Miss Black says calmly as she pulls out the papers and slides them towards us on the desk.

Mel nearly chokes, but recovers quickly and doesn't look up at me. She groans, like she doesn't want to go, and leans back in her chair. "He's one messed up piece of work, Miss Black."

"I realize that, but he requested both of you and said he was impressed with your previous services. The fee was quite high, but he paid it, so maybe you won't mind so much." She winks at Mel and slips a piece of paper toward her.

Mel is in the middle of a sentence by the time she picks up the paper. "No amount of money could make me want to go back to that guy's... Holy shit. Are you for real?" Mel can act, that's for sure. She looks completely surprised.

Black smiles serenely. "Yes, so let him do whatever he wants."

"Done," Mel sits up and grabs a pen. "Where do I sign?" Miss Black points and Mel scribbles her name.

"These are for next week. More of the regular." Black hands the papers to Mel and she signs up for a few more appointments. "And Miss Stanz, here are your clients." She pushes a paper toward me. They're names, not contracts, because I no longer get to agree to anything. I go where she tells me, and do whatever the guy wants. I don't take the paper.

Taking a deep breath, I stiffen and stand my ground. "I was serious, Miss Black. I can't do this anymore. Mr. Ferro is my last client." Suddenly, I have no idea what to do with my hands so I fold them over my chest.

Miss Black smiles at me. She's seated at the table across from Mel, with her long lean legs crossed at the knee with one foot bobbing up and down. She taps the pen once on the paper. "I see. And there's nothing I can do to change your mind?"

"No."

"No amount of money will make it more enticing for you to stay?" Mel watches the exchange without comment, but her head turns side to side like a dog watching a tennis ball.

Fear prickles my skin, but my voice is firm. "It's not about money. I can't do it anymore. I'm not cut out for this."

Miss Black grins tightly before looking over at Mel. "Well, we can't make you stay,

Miss Stanz. Although we strongly encourage it." There's something menacing in her tone. It completely contradicts the light smile on her lips.

I glance at Mel, but she seems just as surprised as I am. Stepping over to Black, I ask, "What are you saying?"

Miss Black stands so we're eye to eye. Her gaze is intimidating, but I don't look away and I won't back up. When Black speaks, she's so close that her minty breath washes over my face. "That your life will be better if you work here and worse if you choose to leave." Her mouth hugs each word tightly, like it's a simple statement and nothing more. A smile spreads across her face that instantly sends a jolt of ice down my spine.

Gabe told me to get out of here as fast as I can. I'm out of options. She's not letting me quit and talking is getting me nowhere. I wish I could say something else, but nothing comes to mind. The only way out is to agree with her, so that's what I do. "Maybe you're right. Maybe more money will make it more tolerable." My gaze drops to the floor and

Miss Black beams at me, and touches my shoulder lightly.

"Excellent. I knew I could count on you, Avery. We are going to be very rich women when this is over. Just wait. Your dream of being a marriage therapist will seem trite in comparison."

Her words are like barbs. Each one is shot with precision directly into me. Her intention is to belittle my dreams and show me that I can have everything if I stay with her. Black knows she's losing me, that I don't want to be here anymore, so she's throwing logic in my face. It's difficult to ignore her when she makes so much sense. I've worked my ass off for my degree. It's a piece of paper that will allow me to get another piece of paper that will allow me to finally become what I always wanted to be. When I was younger, I could see myself in a big old house with a little office around on the side. There was a husband and a baby inside. They were dreams and I was content with the thought of middle class life, and trying to get by like everyone else.

But what she just said, the things she is offering, make those dreams seem so fragile.

I've been walking on cracking ice for a while now, and it's been growing thinner and thinner. One misstep will destroy everything. Somehow the certainties that I once held have all been snatched away. One rumor, one wrong place at the wrong time, or one accusation could ruin me and I'd be worse off than I am now. Alone, I'd have no way to support myself. Every issue of my life could stabilize if I say yes and continue to work here. I could have my own fortune, and I wouldn't be subject to the whims of other people. That's what Black's offering and it makes so much sense that it hurts. She knew exactly what to say, where to strike.

For a second, I look at Black. My words are meant to find a soft spot in her armor, a longing for a life she let slip away. "What were your dreams when you were my age? What did you want to be, Miss Black?" My tone implies that there was no way she chose this job, but the look on her face says otherwise.

Stepping towards me, her voice takes on a caring tone that sounds too motherly to be coming from her mouth. "I dreamt of power, and was willing to do anything necessary to secure my future. You'd be foolish if you don't do the same. In the end, the only person you can depend on is you. People come and go, they're born and die. The only constant in your life is you."

Numbness spreads through me like poison, lurching from my fingertips to my toes. I can barely move. Black has found something that terrifies me more than small spaces, and this time when an imaginary coffin flashes before my eyes, I'm not trapped in it.

Instead, I'm in a funeral home and looking down at Sean.

CHAPTER 7

I'm not normal anymore. At one time I might have been mainstream, but not now. There are too many nightmares that walk about in daylight, and Black just pinpointed my worst fear. I barely survived my parents' deaths. I couldn't make it through Sean's, and yet, everyone must die. It's a matter of when and how much time we have left. I don't suppose other people think about death the way I do. Sometimes I imagine the worst thing possible, trying to brace myself for it, so I never feel so off balance again.

The day my parents died was unexpected. There was nothing to brace me, no one to hold me up. At times like that a person finds out how strong they are, and I've started to think that I am not weak. I endured it and I can still smile. I lived through tragedy and still breathe. I got to tomorrow and things looked brighter, but Black saying that—suggesting that one day I'll be alone again—cut me to the core. She found my weakness.

We leave the building without another word. Gabe has the limo waiting out front, so Mel and I slip inside and get out of the chilly night air. Sighing, I lean my head back against the seat as Gabe drives us in silence.

Mel finally speaks, "Don't let her get inside your head. That's what she was trying to do, Avery. Shove her out."

I wish it were that simple, but Black's words planted a seed in my mind. The thought is already growing, vining around inside my head like a rampant weed. I don't want it there, but she spoke the truth. The thought of losing Sean terrifies me. I can't go back to that life where I was barely glued together. I'm not strong enough to live through it again. "I know, but she knew what she was doing and honed in on something that scares me more than anything. The stupid thing is that I had no idea it was there. I mean, I always said my biggest fear was being trapped inside a closet or something. She blindsided me, that's all, and it would have been easier to blow her off if it wasn't the truth."

"People weave the truth into lies all the time, Avery. It's the best way to bring someone down, and that's what Black's trying to do to you." Mel glances up at Gabe. Her eyes shift away from him, like maybe she shouldn't be saying these things in front of him.

"Gabe won't repeat anything. Say whatever you're thinking." I slouch back in the seat, trying to keep my butt from peeking out from under my way-too-short dress.

Gabe glances back at us and nods once. "I don't hear nothin'." He stares ahead at the traffic.

"First of all, I feel guilty. I had no idea things were going to turn out like this. I'm sorry, Avery. I really am. And no matter what she says, no matter what she tells you, don't wade deeper into this shit than you already are. You'll never get out, and that's what she wants. I have no idea why, but Black wants you. It's personal. If you give in and stay, you'll never get out."

I'm staring at the floor while she speaks. Mel has a good point, and I want to tell her she's right so that she'll stop worrying about me. "Mel, I'm not going back after tonight. This is the last time."

"Avery," there's a warning tone in her voice, "You can't blow off Black like that."

Glancing at her out of the corner of my eye, I ask, "Then how do I quit, Mel?"

"I don't know. Right now you have too many clients asking for you. She knows how much you're worth and what it means to lose you. You're irreplaceable in her head. She said as much tonight." I give her a weird look because I didn't think she heard that part of our conversation. Mel wasn't there for most of it. She rolls her eyes and huffs. "I was listening outside the door, okay? I told you that I was at Black's and I was. I just wasn't in her office yet."

"What were you doing?" By the sound of it, Mel was doing something she shouldn't have been.

She shakes her head. "Nothing that you need to know about. You're in enough trouble, but let's just say I overheard some of the things she said to you in private, all right, and I don't like this Avery." Mel shivers and rubs her hands over her arms. "Something's not right, not anymore. I mean, getting that many requests is strange. Your price goes sky high and they back off or leave because they can't afford you. Where the hell are these guys getting their money? You should be unattainable by now."

"Maybe Black made the whole thing up and the only guy asking for me over and over again is Sean."

She nods and touches her finger to her lips, unblinking. "Black's never said that to me, but then again, I haven't tried to leave."

For a second, I'm afraid that she still feels guilty. I can't read her when she's so still and quiet. "There's no way you could have known."

She nods again, slowly bobbing her head up and down, still dazed. Gabe drops us off at the front of the hotel and drives away. Mel and I walk across the lobby without a word. There are so many eyes on me, sizing me up, and wondering what kind of slut I am to be wearing this dress. It makes my pulse race faster, but I manage to hold onto my confident stance and keep my head held high. This is a game, this façade isn't who I am, it's an illusion.

Mel and I ride the elevator to Sean's floor before we step off and head down the hall. That's when a gush of words erupts from Mel's mouth. "I was wrong, so goddamn wrong to pull you into this. I said she wasn't a pimp, that she didn't do shit like this, and here she is doing it. Avery, I swear to God—"

Mel's voice is strained and her eyes have that vacant stare that so often accompanies guilt. This isn't her fault, no matter what happens, I'll never blame her. I stop abruptly, grab Mel's shoulders and look her in the eye. "There is no way you knew that Black was like this. I believe you. You're not responsible for whatever happens next. I'm the one who agreed to come, I'm the one who signed up to be this, and I'm the one who will have to deal with the consequences. It's not your fault Mel."

Her gaze falls to the side, like she can't look me in the eye, which is weird for Mel. "I took you there and said it was safe. I screwed up, Avery." She's mad at herself and upset for me. There's no telling what will happen or how hard it will be to defy Black, but no matter what happens, it's not her fault. This was my doing, not hers.

"Mel, that night you asked me to go and meet your boss, I could have said no, and I didn't. After I found out what the job was, I could have said no. I had the opportunity to say no and walk away so many times. The fact is, I took the job and nothing you said made me do it. Everything will be fine. Don't worry about it."

That's a big fat lie. I have no idea how everything will work out. It feels like I have a pack of pissed off people snarling and circling. Black can lunge at me with her fangs bared at any time. With my luck, it'll be tomorrow.

Sean's voice comes from over my shoulder. "Don't worry about what?"

CHAPTER 8

When I turn around, his eyes ravish me, boldly lingering in places they shouldn't. I smack his chest and scold him, "Stop it!"

Sean grins so hard that dimples appear on his cheek. Oh God. They're like little lickable magnets and they're pulling me in. He could recite a poem about water buffaloes right now and I'd have no idea what he'd said.

Sean presses his finger to the end of my nose, making me blink. "If you didn't want me to look, then you shouldn't have worn that dress."

"I didn't. Black made me change."

His smile broadens. "Then, this should be fun." He takes my hand and presses a kiss to the back of my palm, making butterflies erupt in my stomach. It's a school girl response and although I try to squash it, I still giggle. Sean's smirk changes slightly, but he doesn't take his eyes off of me. Holding out his other hand to Mel, he says, "Come along ladies. I have our night all planned out."

Mel gives me a weird look and slips her palm into his. We follow Sean into the room and let the door close behind us. Sean drops Mel's hand and squeezes mine once before letting go. "Avery, I need to talk to you about earlier, but from the sound of it, I already know what's happening."

"What do you mean?" Mel asks, as she sits down on the chair by the desk. "What happened earlier?"

"One of Black's guys saw us together," Sean explains. "Gabe showed up and warned Avery before things got ugly. Your employer thought you girls were dishing out on the side."

"No, I don't think that's the problem," I explain. "Black's doing something. I tried to quit tonight and she wouldn't let me."

"Tell me what happened, and don't leave a thing out." Sean leans against the wall and folds his arms over his chest. He's wearing a dark suit with the shirt still buttoned up to his neck and a blackish blue tie. It looks like he was at work, either that or he dressed up for the occasion, which is laughable since he said he was giving us a night off. When I get to the end of my story, Sean doesn't move. He stares into space, and the only way I can tell that he's livid is the tightening of his jaw. I'm pretty sure he could bite the head off of a chicken right now.

Mel sighs and looks out the window. She's not stupid enough to mess with Sean when he's about to blow up. Yeah, but I am. I reach for a candy from the mint dish and peg him in the chest. It leaves some powdered sugar on my fingers so I suck it off and then grab another one. "These are good."

"Avery, stop." Sean inhales slow and deep.

I don't mention the last words Black said to me or the conversation with Mel in the car. That'd be too much for him, and it worries me. Sean doesn't know what he does to me or how attached I've become, but Black sees it. I try to make light of the situation to diffuse some of his tension. "Sean, it's not so bad. I just have to get out of it and make her not want me anymore. I planned on not showing up but Mel said that was—"

"A stupid idea," Mel finishes my sentence for me.

"Yeah, so I guess I need to move onto plan B and figure out how to get fired." I shrug and turn back to the mint jar. Where is all this false confidence coming from? Two seconds ago, I felt like I couldn't deal with Black and now I'm talking about manipulating her into firing my ass like it's nothing.

Sean steps up behind me. I feel his warm breath wash over my shoulder. God, he smells good. "So, you want to stop working for Black?"

Turning, I look up at him, and nod. "Yeah, it turns out that I still have a heart and it's somewhere else."

Sean tries not to smile. "So, were you going to say yes, Miss Smith?"

"It depends on what you were going to ask me, Mr. Jones." I'm looking into his eyes and wondering if we can have a future together. I want it more than anything, but I don't know. There are so many obstacles in the way, and we both have so much baggage. It seems impossible, but when Sean's with me, it doesn't feel that way.

Mel gags herself and slams her head on the desk. Sean and I stare at her. When she lifts her head, she scolds us. "People, share that lovey-dovey shit some other time. We have problems right now." She taps her finger firmly on the desk for emphasis.

Sean clears his throat and steps away from me, like he was caught doing something wrong. As if showing affection is a criminal offense. "So, let me make sure I understand what you want to do, Avery. You're plan is to go into Black's, take the clients, and be so horrible that they don't want you again?" His dark brow lifts, but he manages to ask without laughing or strangling me.

Mel rolls her eyes and says, "Yes," at the same time I say, "No!"

They both look at me. I sigh dramatically and kick off my heels before pacing and talking with my hands. They're flying everywhere. "I won't sleep with them. I'll be so revolting that we won't get that far. They'll throw me out, and demand a refund. Last time someone refused me, she wanted to fire me—so it should work this time, right?"

"Last time you did that, Black didn't think you were running your own brothel. Besides, I can't let you do that." Sean is staring at me. His arms are folded together and I realize that he never talks with his hands. I'm pretty sure that if I couldn't move while I was talking, I'd fall over.

"The other option is to not show up."

Mel shakes her head. "Black will hunt you down to make sure you're not dead in a gutter or something. You can't no-show. And when she finds you alive, you'll wish you were dead." There's a moment of silence and then Mel finally asks, "Why'd you two add me to your little freak show tonight? I mean, I wasn't going to ask. I was just going to wait and see, but no one has said anything and I'm out of patience."

Jabbing my thumb at Sean, I tell her, "He's giving us a night off."

"No way." Mel's perfect eyebrows lift in surprise.

"Way."

"Well, then…" Mel kicks off her heels, and takes off her earrings and lays them on the desk, before adding, "I'm really glad, because I wasn't looking forward to seeing Avery's boney ass."

"Ha!" I turn to Sean with my jaw hanging open and my finger pointing at Mel. "I told you that she didn't like me!"

Sean shrugs like he wasn't all that committed to the idea. Mel watches us before blurting out, "What the fuck are you two talking about, because if you think I'm gay because I'm a good friend, I might have to beat the shit out of you, scary Ferro reputation or not."

Sean holds up his hands, palms toward her. "No offense meant. I just noticed how much she means to you and thought there might have been more there."

"There's not, you bunch of white toast with…" Mel sputters, trying to find the right insult, before giving up. Her hands slap the table. "You're so dumb, you know that? Just 'cuz I'm a hooker doesn't mean I do everyone and everything."

"What's your type?" Sean asks abruptly.

"Rich." Mel's shoulders are back and tension lines her arms. It's like she's ready to fight, but I have no idea what set her off. She sleeps with guys and didn't object to the idea of having a woman, assuming she's loaded. Sean watches my friend, waiting for a real answer, but there's no way in hell that she'll tell him anything. Come to think of it, I've never heard much about her hopes and dreams, only that she doesn't want to go back to the hellhole she climbed out of.

Mel rolls her eyes and laughs. The tension dissipates as she points at Sean. "And not you, Ferro. You're way too fucked up for me. And this conversation is officially over. I'm gonna eat me some noodles. What do you guys say to take-out?"

"Actually, I have other plans for Avery and I." Sean's voice sounds scary, the way it does when he's anxious. He looks down at me, "We have a table downstairs."

I can't help it and crack a smile. "Really?"

He nods. "Yes, there was something I needed to ask you earlier and I didn't get the chance."

I try not to show any emotion, but I can't. I giggle and try so hard not to jump up and down. "I love this game!"

Mel groans, "Oh my God. Get out of here. You two make me sick."

Sean smiles deeply and tosses Mel a room service menu. "Order anything you like."

Mel is leaning her elbow on the desk and has her head in her hand. "Can I get another hooker, so I have someone to play chess with?"

If Sean's shocked, he hides it well. His voice is flat. "No."

"You're no fun," Mel pouts.

"I already hired two call girls for one evening. Many people would say that's more than enough fun for one man."

"Psh, whatever White Boy. Go play house with Avery. I'm going to order crab cakes and the seafood buffet for six people."

I lean in towards Sean, "You're going to need to order another room since this one will smell like fish."

Sean laughs and takes my hands. "Order anything you like, Mel. I mean it. Come on, Avery. Our table awaits."

Before we walk out of the room, Mel asks, "What about Black?"

Sean looks back at her, and then narrows his gaze in my direction. "There's a more pressing question to be asked first, especially since it will demand a different response to your question of employment."

CHAPTER 9

Every inch of my body is giddy with excitement. It's to the point that I'm shaking and I can't shut up. Ever since we stepped out of the room, I can't stop smiling or talking. I take Sean's hand and lean against his shoulder in the elevator. "Ask me," I whisper, but there are other people in the small space. I know he won't, but it's fun to tease him.

Sean looks down at me from the corner of his eyes. He's got that stern formal thing going on and I wish he'd slouch just a little bit. He can't be nervous, can he? Surely Sean knows what I'm going to say. "You're awfully quiet, Mr. Ferro."

The couple standing across from us looks displeased. The woman's face visibly contorts and her polished appearance isn't enough to distract from her disgust. Sean sees it and tightens his jaw, but he says nothing.

The man standing with her looks unimpressed, and scoots closer to the woman, like Sean might go all cray cray on their pampered asses, and kill everyone before the elevator reaches the ground floor. I hate it. I hate the way they look at Sean, like he's soulless. Sean Ferro is not a monster.

I don't know what comes over me, but I can't bite my tongue. I blurt it out. "Don't look at him like that."

The woman sneers at me. "Just because he's wealthy doesn't mean he should get away with murder. It was a massive injustice to Amanda Ferro and her family, and you are a fool to be standing so close to him."

Sean doesn't respond, he just stands there with his hands clasped in front of him, waiting for the doors to open. I don't understand why he doesn't fight back. They're rude, and wrong.

Screw it. I step toward the woman and look her in the eye. "You don't know a thing about Amanda or Sean Ferro, and you're an idiot if you think everything you see on TV is true."

Her jaw drops open and the man standing next to her pulls her closer, increasing the distance between us. His jaw opens like he's going to say something, but the DING cuts him off and the doors open.

I take Sean's hand and give them a lethal look as we walk out. "Stupidity is for the weak-minded, and you better not sit by us."

Sean pulls me away and tucks my hand under his arm. He takes a deep breath. "Avery, you can't yell at every person who hates me. First of all, the list is endless, and second, you can't convince them of something they don't want to hear." Sean's blue gaze rests on the side of my face and there's something there, like he's accepted this horrible public persona.

"Yeah, well...They're stupid." I'm a genius! That's the problem, everyone else is dumb. People see what they want to see and nothing more. Everyone knows that the media is biased. They all hated that Sean didn't cry, that he seemed inhuman during the trial. He's more human than they realize, breakable like everyone else, but who wants to report on that? The idea that Sean Ferro is a monster sells better.

Sean's voice is warm and kind. "They prefer to think of me as a villain. I've learned to live with it, the question is, can you?" He smiles softly and takes my hand as we reach the restaurant doors.

A smirk appears on my lips. I don't want to drop this injustice, but Sean brings up the question again. I poke his chest, right over his heart. "That better not be what you were going to ask me."

Sean's eyes glitter, like he's trying not to laugh. I love it when he's like this. If I could figure out which mixture of annoying and innocent (or naïve) was conjuring that smile, I'd use it all the time.

"This way, Mr. Ferro." The man behind the desk grabs two menus and walks us to the back of the room, past staring eyes, and to a perfect little table—the table where we had our first meal together. Awh.

I glance up at him as I sit in my chair. "Did you pick this table on purpose, Mr. Ferro?"

"I do everything on purpose." Sean settles back into his chair and rests his hands on the arms like it's a throne.

I mirror his posture. "Me too." Sean laughs abruptly. I love that sound and the way he leans forward like it's a horrible thing to witness. "Honestly, Mr. Ferro, I have no idea what you're laughing about." My voice is light, and teasing. "I'm a very intentional person, it's just that my best intentions usually go awry."

He laughs louder and actually twists in his seat. "Avery, you are a spectacular woman, but I cannot possibly imagine a world where you deliberately let your car be stolen, and then flashed traffic to jump on the back of a stranger's bike."

Grinning at him, I lift my water glass and take a sip before saying smugly, "I planned the whole thing. You fell into my elaborate trap." I offer a soft, diabolical laugh and smirk at him.

Sean leans forward and takes my hands. "Do you ever wonder if you fell into mine?"

I make a face. "That wasn't the right question, either. Ask me, Mr. Ferro."

Sean is cradling my hands in his and staring into my eyes. My pulse races faster when he looks at me like that. He has this hypnotic stare that's unnerving, and sexy as hell. Sean's eyes dip to the table and then back to my face. My heart pounds harder and I can't stop smiling. Part of me wants to squee up and down the hallway, but I need to act sane for a moment.

Sean's lips part and I'm ready. My answer is ready. I'm so excited!

His eyes dip to the table. "Avery, I can't ask you now."

CHAPTER 10

I blink. "Rich boy say what?"

He pats my hands and tips his head to the side. "Stop talking like a cartoon character, and listen. I wanted things to be a certain way, at a specific time. You'll have to wait." He pulls his hands away and leans back in his chair.

My bottom lip curls out and I'm pouting without meaning to. "I hate waiting."

Sean just grins in response. He doesn't produce the ring or mention marriage.

There's no talk like before, at the beach, no nothing. He's stern and cold again. I don't hide my disappointment. I can't. It feels like I've been sucker punched one too many times and I can no longer pretend not to care. Sean ordered before we ever sat down. It would have irritated me if he didn't get the most delicious food I'd ever put in my mouth. Sean is presumptive and it pisses me off, because this thing with the ring and the food, it's to show how well he knows me and how well he can control me. Yeah, I want things like that sometimes, but not now.

After dinner, I'm leaning pretty far to my right, with my elbow on the table and my hand holding up my head. Think surly teenager. It's not pretty but after this morning, I expected more from him. Sean has issues. Every time I feel like we're on the same page, he does something like this. I'd cry if I weren't so pissed off.

The waiter brings out our desserts and refills my champagne glass. For a moment, I wonder if he's going to propose during dessert like a normal guy, but Sean would never hide the ring in something. He's too straightforward for that. Since there's no jewelry in sight, I'm doubting that there's going to be a proposal tonight.

I poke at my dessert, but don't really eat it. Sean notices. "Are you finished?" He's been watching me from the other side of the table, quieter than usual. Or maybe I'm just steaming too much to be a good date.

"Yes," I say, pushing away the plate. The truth is I'm a little crushed and feeling the post-Christmas crash, but I didn't get any presents. It sucks monkeys. I can't even pretend anymore. I glance around the room and wonder if anyone else is having a crappy night. The other couples look happy, like they're celebrating something special. This place cost a small fortune, so it's a treat to eat here. A bunch of the patrons probably blew a week's pay on this dinner. Except for my man, Sean. He's got lots of money and even more emotional PMS. God, he's worse than I am. Maybe.

"Good, because I have a question for you." I straighten in my seat a little bit and try not to let my balloon of hope inflate again. Seriously, that thing has been bent every which way and resembles a deflated knot right about now. Sean puts his fork down and folds his hands together. "Are you attending your graduation ceremony?"

My face scrunches up. "What?" Weird question.

"They asked me to give a lecture to the graduating class—to be the guest speaker—and I told them that I'd have to ask you."

I lean on my elbow again and pick at the table cloth. "I wasn't planning on it."

"Why not?"

"There's no one to hood me. You know, before you walk across the stage, someone puts the sashie thing over your head and rests it on your shoulders. My mom would have done it. Since she's not here, I figured..." I look up into his face and see the fragility. Looking back down at the table, I say, "I don't understand. Why do you want to hood me? You know you don't actually get to tie me up, right?"

He nods, but doesn't smile. Actually, it looks like I kicked him. "I know."

"Then why?" I watch Sean as he taps his finger on the table and avoids my gaze.

"Because you sacrificed everything for that moment. If this isn't fleeting, if I matter to you—"

Straightening in my seat, I finally say what I'm thinking. "Sean, why won't you ask me?" He looks away and doesn't answer. This isn't a game anymore. I think he had every intention of asking me when we were upstairs, but something changed. There's no pressing need to ask me anything. Sean's sitting there like he always does. I try to stay calm and ask the question even though I already know the answer. "Did you change your mind?"

His blue gaze flicks up and meets mine. "No."

Liar. "Just tell me the truth. Don't hide behind that placid expression and let yourself feel for a second."

"Let myself feel? Do you seriously think that's the problem?"

"Not in its entirety, but I think a general lack of empathy is part of the problem." That was a cheap shot, but it infuriates me when he acts so stoic. He can act that way with everyone else, but not with me.

Sean mashes his mouth shut and looks back and forth before leaning forward and blasting me. "Do you know what they're going to say about you if you become Mrs. Sean Ferro? Do you seriously think that I haven't thought about it? About how you'd take it when those insults are hurled at you? Avery, I've heard so many hateful things, day after day. I wish I could tell you that I don't care, that they roll off like rain, but they don't. You haven't had to endure that kind of punishment and you've done nothing to warrant it, but marrying me will be enough. People will talk, they'll be unkind toward you, and it will be my fault. If you carry my name, you carry my burdens." He pats his napkin to his lips and looks like he just opened a checking account. There's no emotion in those blue eyes, they're vacant of grief and pain.

The hollow spot inside my chest constricts as I look away. He isn't going to ask me. That little altercation in the elevator made him change his mind. Sean doesn't think I can handle it. I'm not going to cry. Screw that. The center of my chest aches so badly that I speak without thinking. "So what, you don't trust me with those burdens?"

"No, I want to save you from them. Unkind words are the nicest things that happen to me, Avery." Sean acts like he wants to say more, but he doesn't. He just sits there in his chair like it's a goddamn throne and watches me.

Maybe I could have accepted this a few weeks ago, but not now. If I get up and walk away, it'll be the end of it. Sean won't follow me. I smile at him as every hope dissolves inside my chest. I haven't the words to tell him what he's done to me, exactly what level of hell he just tossed me into.

So I say nothing. I simply stand, toss my napkin on the table, and walk away. I should have known better than to think Sean Ferro would actually ask me to share his life.

CHAPTER 11

That man took my heart and shredded it. I've walked away and there's no going back. I don't expect him to follow me or say a damn thing. He's weird like that. He usually lets me wander off, swearing under my breath, and then shows up after I calm down. But not this time. Sean's arm juts between the elevator doors as they close. "Avery, wait."

The hollow feeling inside my chest is overflowing with pain and dripping into my shoes. I can't look at him and pretend it doesn't hurt. I'm a moron. I keep thinking the best of people. I never learn. I don't say anything. I don't look up.

He steps inside and we're alone. The elevator starts to move upward toward our floor when Sean steps in front of the panel and pulls the STOP. We lurch to a halt and my heart tries to tear out of my chest. Panic makes my eyes dart around the dark little room as my palms slam backward into the wall, grasping at the rail like it can save me. I hate small spaces, and being trapped in an elevator is as bad as being nailed into a coffin. Sean knows that.

He finds me in the dim emergency lighting and slips his hands around my waist and tugs me to him. I try to pull away, but he won't let me. Sean's grip on me tightens and he pins me to the wall. "Never walk away from me again. You can be angry, but you can't be indifferent."

"You are!"

"I am not," he's close to growling. I can tell that I'm poking every button he has, but I'm tired of his games. Every time we get closer, he turns and runs. It's driving me crazy, and since I'm already certifiable, I'm not handling it gracefully.

"You are so! You don't care about me. I'm just another trinket to you—something to own and play with. I don't matter to you!"

"Avery, I'd give my life for you. Why can't you understand that I can't have what I want either? I want you to be my wife. I want what you want. Do you hear me? I want to marry you. I want you in every conceivable means, but I can't be so callous. It'll destroy you, my love, and I can't do that." His hands are in my hair and I can feel his hard body against mine.

I can barely speak, my throat is so tight. This tiny box is suffocating me to the point that I'm thinking about clawing at the walls. But his words cut through the fear and I hear his concern, even if I still don't understand. "You didn't have to stop the elevator."

"I'm sorry. I knew you wouldn't listen otherwise. Avery, I want a life for us—one with the little house and the picket fence— but that's not what's in store for me. I am the Ferro they fear most and they have every right to act that way. My hands aren't clean, Avery. I'm not above reproach, and I have too many enemies. Things will never be so simple. God, and if you took my name, if they knew about you…" His voice trails off and he sighs deeply, burying his face in the curve between my neck and shoulder. Hot breath spills across my skin, raising goose bumps.

My entire body is strung tight, but his lips where they are make my stomach twist and tingle. Maybe it's fear that makes me think of his mouth on me, doing sinful things, but the thought of wrapping my legs around his hips blazes through my mind. The moment is charged with tension and vulnerability, at least it is for me. I press my lips together several times, before I can manage the words. "Ask me. Give me the chance to choose my life."

As the words pour from my lips, I reach for him and splay my hands on his chest, under the lapel of his jacket. My heart is beating so hard, so fast. I think about his mouth on mine and hot kisses, but worry is holding me back.

"I can't do that to you." Sean tenses when I touch him, but he doesn't push me away. Instead he holds me tighter, dipping his hands lower, past my waist.

"Do you have any idea what it does to me when you stop this thing? Every thought in my head is telling me that I'm going to die if we don't move, but I'm shoving past it because I know I'm safe with you, Sean." My hands are splayed on his chest and I can feel the rapid beating of his heart. Sean's passion runs deep, and his worries are real. I can't deny that, but we can't stay like this forever. "I know the world is unkind. I know what it means to be alone, and I'm not leaving here without you realizing that. A life without you is so much worse than anything someone might do to me."

Reaching around his waist, I pull at his shirt, freeing it from his waistband. Sean tenses, his spine straightening, as I move my hands up under the hem of his shirt and trail my fingers over his hard stomach. He's facing me. It's the way I dream of being with him, of touching him, but Sean doesn't typically allow it. In this moment, the world is dumped on its head. If I can tolerate being trapped in a warm box with no light or air, then he can bear my touch, and he does.

Sean is quiet for a moment and I can feel the tension in his taut muscles. He's so still, except for the slow, deliberate breaths that fill his lungs. People breathe like that when they're afraid. I know because I'm doing the same thing.

"It's not a question of *if*, but *when*." His voice shudders as I trail my palms across his body, tracing the lines of his torso. His skin is so hot. If I wasn't wearing a dress, if I could press my naked body to his, I'd die. For a second I understand his sexual draw to fear and how it mingles with lust, because it's there and incredibly difficult to ignore.

Sean's voice is a whisper. "I can't knowingly do something that will hurt you. I can't let them—" He shivers and presses his hips to mine, showing me exactly how he feels. When he pulls away, I'm breathless. "Avery, you know what you do to me, and how I feel about you. If you weren't wearing panties, I'd have that dress hiked up and take you right here and now."

Leaning in close, my lips brush against his ear as I whisper, "Then, I'm afraid I'll have to hold you to your word, right after you ask me something I really want to hear."

Sean makes a noise at the back of his throat before dipping his hands lower, cupping my butt and feeling for verification of my statement. His words come out in a raspy breath. "This isn't fair. You know my weakness—that it's a fantasy to have you like this, here."

I'm playing with fire, tempting fate, and being utterly reckless. Sean's concerns are valid, but I can't help feeling like I should have some say in what happens to us. "You should let me decide whether or not I can handle sharing your life."

CHAPTER 12

He's torn, I can hear it in his heavy breaths. Sean could pull away and start the elevator, but I know how turned on he is, how much he wants me. I didn't do it on purpose and he's the one who stopped the thing, but I have to push him. He can't act like he's protecting me when his actions are killing me inside.

Sean slams his hands on the wall behind my head and pulls away. "We can't! You can barely handle your own life. Damn it, Avery. I can hardly hold it together anymore, and you're the living proof that I've lost my fucking mind. I can't have the life you want. It's not mine to offer you. I'm sorry."

"Sean—" I grasp at him, not wanting him to pull further away from me, but he does. A rush of cold air fills the space where he stood.

"Tell me. Tell me, if you know. If you can see how to get there from here, to that place where you and I could have what my brother, Pete, has. If you can see the path, I'll ask you. If you can tell me how we crawl out of this hell, I'll do it. I'd do anything for you, be anything for you, but I can't figure it out." He's back in front of me, so close, but he doesn't reach for me.

"Sean, you don't have to do it alone. Sometimes it takes two people to fix things. And sometimes, you have to trust blindly and jump." Panic is rising up my throat and it feels like there's a massive pile of bricks on my chest, but I manage to hold back the scream, and the tears.

Claustrophobia wasn't much of an issue until my parents died, and then it got worse. I hate elevators and tiny spaces. They freak me out, and while I might be standing with a pleasant expression on my face, I'm really praying to God that we don't get stuck. Now that I am stuck, it takes every ounce of sanity within me to control the fear, but it doesn't want to be tamed. It's snarling and animalistic, ready to claw out of here. Still, I push it down and keep the terror in check. I don't let my emotions overtake me.

Instead, I reach for Sean, pulling at his belt until he crushes me into the wall with his body. I hold him to me, feeling the smooth skin on his back and those hot muscles, before reaching for his pants. Sean's voice is gone. He's all hot breath and powerful hands. He realizes what I'm doing and can't hold back. As I free him from his slacks, he hikes up the hem of my dress pushing it up past my hips.

Sean's lips come crashing down on mine, hot and perfect. His kiss is wild, demanding and devouring. As his lips slip to my neck, he dips his hand between my legs, pressing between my thighs. My body is in emotional overload. The faster I breathe, the hotter it gets. The warmer I am, the more afraid I become. The room shrinks with each gasp, but I want him. It's a strange sensation, caught between lust and fear, and I can't control myself. Tears streak my face, but there's a smile on my lips. I'm insane. That's got to be what's wrong with me, because I almost like this. It's intense, and all consuming.

Sean lifts me and presses my back against the wall. His strong hands grip my upper thighs as I wrap my legs around his hips. Sweat drips down my temples as Sean slowly pushes into me and my head slams back into the wall. There's no air, no light. My mind tells me I'm dying, but my body is climbing higher and higher, tingling with that insatiable feeling that's delicious torture. Sean's thrusts start out slow and rhythmic. He doesn't speak and I wonder if I'm going to pass out. It's so hot and the air is so still. My mind is screaming like there's a pillow obstructing my face, but the delicious pulsing between my legs keeps me sane. Sean slams into me harder and faster, rocking us higher and higher. I hear myself sob and don't know why. I don't understand the tears or the terror that's coursing through me, but when I feel him between my legs, when Sean loses it and shoves into me that final time before he stills, I feel perfect, and my body responds and shatters. My nails bite into his skin as I cry out and feel the release.

The high from this is different, and I don't know what to think. I can't think. My body doesn't know what I'm doing, or how it should react. I'm not sad, even though I shudder in his arms and tears streak my cheeks. My heart is pounding at the aftershocks and I can barely breathe, but it's hard to tell if it's from fear or euphoria.

I stay there like that, pressed to the wall with him still inside of me. Sean's hands grip my thighs and his thumbs rub little circles on my skin. Neither of us says anything for a moment. I don't want to move, but I can't hold my legs around him any longer. They start shaking, so Sean pulls out and puts me down. My knees nearly buckle and my entire body is trembling, but I manage to pull the hem of my dress back down.

I hear Sean moving, redressing himself, before the lights come back on. They flicker, making me blink several times. As soon as his eyes adjust, he turns to look at me. Sean is pristine in his suit without a wrinkle on him. Meanwhile, I look and feel like a total mess. I'm covered in sweat and can barely stand.

For a moment we just watch each other. Then Sean finally says, "I can't believe you did that for me."

I lean back against the wall, and clutch the bar so I don't fall over. I don't trust myself to speak. Sean smiles at me and nods, before turning to the control panel again. I'm afraid he's going to stop it and I can't manage to be in here for another second. As it is, I'm going to need therapy after this, so I lunge for him. "No, please. I can't."

But Sean's already done what he wanted. He pressed every button for every floor and then turns to me, smiling wide. "I needed more time, because I have something I need to tell you." Sean tucks his chin and steps over to me, with his hands in his pockets. It's such a boyish gesture, and so was pressing all the buttons, that I have no idea what he wants to do. The doors open and fresh air hits my face, calming me.

An irritated hotel employee is standing there with a crowd of people behind him.

He's saying something, but Sean ignores him. I take a deep breath before the doors slip shut again.

"Avery, I'm selfish. I've always been that way and what you just did was so completely..." he sucks in air and shakes his head. "There are no words. You give everything you have. You don't hold back, and by God, if I could be like you for even a moment, if I could have your strength, your courage, your conviction—I can't even fathom it." The elevator is stopping floor by floor as he speaks. Sean doesn't pause. He doesn't look at the people waiting outside in the hallway, people who don't want to get onto the broken elevator with the monologuing man.

The doors close and the pattern repeats until a little old lady gets on with us. She looks at me and then Sean, and smiles at his words. She's wearing a pink paisley dress, with a matching pink satin bowling jacket that says RONKONKOMA SEXY DEVILS across the back, with an evening bag under her arm.

She reaches into it and hands me a tissue. "I think he's going to ask you something, dear." The old woman smiles, like this is the highlight of her night.

I take the tissue and dab my eyes. "Thank you, but you're mistaken." I don't look at either of them and try to keep my gaze on the floor.

That's when Sean drops to one knee and holds up a ring to me. "She's not mistaken, and neither were you. I should have asked you. I should have said it sooner, and I wish I could say it better. Avery Stanz, will you marry me? Will you be my wife and share my life? Will you let me love you in sickness and in health? Will you let me stand beside you for the rest of my life? Because, if you say yes, I will love you with all my heart. I won't withhold myself from you, like I've done for so long. I will protect you and give you everything I have. Will you share my bed, my soul, and my life?"

The doors ding open on another floor and the people smile at the sight. Me with a shocked face, the old lady is grinning and close to clapping, and Sean on his knee holding up a ring. As the doors slip shut, they groan since they won't hear my answer.

It's then that I realize I'm taking too long. My heart is pounding and I'm lost in limbo, caught between reality and dreamland. But I'm awake, and Sean's looking up at me, blinking those bright blue eyes, completely and totally vulnerable.

I find my voice. "You jumped." I sound shocked.

He nods. "I'd do anything for you, Avery. I'll be anything you want, anything you need, no matter what you say, but I hope you say yes." He smiles hard and those dimples flash and disappear.

"Yes. Yes, to all those things." My lips quiver and I start sobbing as I hold out my hand. It's shaking so much that Sean has to take it in his to slide the ring on my finger. When the cold metal touches my hot skin a shiver races over me, and I gasp.

When Sean stands, he takes me in his arms and holds me. The old woman claps and rides the elevator up to our floor with us, chattering excitedly, and wishing us well.

For a second, a bitter thought crosses my mind. "You'd wish those things for us even if he were Sean Ferro?" Sean tenses in my arms. It's reckless, because in this moment his guard is down, and so is mine. If the old woman reacts the way the woman did earlier, I'll cry. I don't know why I said it. Something within me urged me to ask, so I did.

The elderly lady smiles, and touches my arm. "I'd wish every happiness on the two of you, especially if he were Sean Ferro. That man has had more pain in his life than one person could reasonably tolerate, and he's bore it with grace. Everyone deserves a little ray of happiness after so much rain."

CHAPTER 13

Sean presses his lips to the side of my face, covering me in little kisses. I giggle, I can't help it. It feels like I'm floating, as if nothing could ruin this moment. The ring catches my eye, sparkling in the dim light of the elevator. I want to look at it, but I don't want to pull away from Sean. I don't want this moment to end. Something changed today. The walls that Sean erected came crashing down and he finally let me in.

There's nothing between us now and I can't wait to snuggle against him once we get back to the room. It's so hard not to jump up and down. I want to tell everyone and show them the ring. I want to tell them that I was right, that Sean wasn't going to be the one to destroy me. I trusted my gut and I was right. It feels so good. The last few months have tossed me around so much that I didn't know which way was up, but tonight, my feet are on the ground, right where they should be—between Sean Ferro and a crazy old lady who looks like she wants to celebrate with me.

She pulls out her phone and deflates when she can't get a signal. "All my friends are going to be so jealous! I got to see the sweetest proposal I've ever witnessed and they're all sitting in the room." She chortles and holds her phone up, tilting it to the side like that'll help it get some bars. "They're going to blow a gasket when they find out it was Sean Ferro. And you... You are so sweet. I'm going to call you Sweetie."

Sean holds me to his chest, hugging me hard and laughs. "She is sweet, and thoughtful, and completely perfect." He kisses the top of my head and I feel my face flame red, which makes the old lady laugh more.

When the doors open on our floor, we both step out. The old woman stays behind. "Congratulations, you two! I'm going to go tell the girls!" She presses the button for her floor, the doors close, and she disappears.

There's a fairytale smile plastered across my face. I used to wonder how princesses could look like that for so long. It had to be because of the prince. I'm talking about cartoon princesses, of course. When someone draws the perfect man, there's a lot to smile about. Sean is by no means perfect, but he's perfect for me.

Before we take another step, the squawk of a police CB shatters the hallway's stuffy silence. Sean's eyes narrow as his gaze shoots to the end of the hall. They're standing in front of our room.

Instinct takes over and I grab Sean's arm and try to pull him to the stairwell. It's right next to me, but Sean shakes his head. They haven't seen us yet. He shakes his head, and makes a snap decision. Leaning in close, he kisses my cheek, and shoves me into the stairwell as he does it. "Stay out of sight."

Without a word, Sean walks toward the room. I glance through the little rectangle of glass, but I can't see him. I can't leave the hotel without setting off my bracelet, and I can't hang out in the stairwell either. My stomach lurches as I consider why the police are here—what it means. Mel was in the room. Something bad could have happened to her, or worse. Someone reported us, which means someone knows we were here with Sean and what we are.

If the cops are looking for call girls, I look the part. Part of me wants to ignore Sean and walk down the hall. But, I'm not that stupid, so I rush down the flight of stairs and grab the elevator to the lobby. As I pass a large marble table with an oversized floral arrangement, I grab a newspaper and head to one of the posh seats. There are tons of reporters right outside the front doors. Flashes keep going off. I feel so sick. Should I crush the bead on my bracelet? Does this count as danger? Black could be exposed if they find me, but they must have found Mel.

I sit down on a blue velvet arm chair and slouch back like I'm not freaking out. As I ponder whether or not to break the bead, I hear three hotel employees speaking in hushed whispers. "I can't believe it's him, I mean first his wife and now this."

"I know. At least he can't get away with it twice."

The third voice chimes in, "I don't know, people don't have a lot of sympathy for hookers."

My spine goes straight. I can't turn and look at them. The buzzing in my head has grown so loud that I can no longer hear their words. It sounds like they think Sean killed a hooker. That means that the cops were in his room because… Mel's dead?

She can't be. I just saw her. She was fine, but they just said… Oh my God. I can't stand it. I turn around and look at them, unable to hide the emotions as they crawl out of my stomach. My jaw drops. I want to ask them what happened, but if I speak, they'll connect the dots. People saw me and Mel walk in together and my clothes say everything. Even so, I don't want to leave Sean and Mel up there. She has to be fine. It's suddenly so hot inside that I feel like I'm going to hurl.

The air in here is too hot, too stuffy. I can't breathe. My skin is numb and it feels like I'm walking in a bubble of cold mist. I try to exit through the bar, but it's packed and there are people guarding the door, keeping the press out. Worry pinches my brow and I decide to head to the ladies room to give myself time to think. Sean said to leave. I need to leave, but I have to do it without being seen. Too bad everyone and their goddamn dog notices me in this dress! I'm about to push through the bathroom door, when a hand rests on my shoulder.

My elbow flies back and jabs the guy in the gut.

CHAPTER 14

I hear an *oof* sound and spin on my heel. "Leave me—oh God! Gabe."

The old guy makes a face and coughs. "Nice move. Let's get you out of here without being noticed."

"What happened? Where's Mel?"

"Later. First things first. Black sent this. Change, and walk straight out the front door. The car is at the curb." He hands me a little designer overnight bag.

Taking it, I nod and push into the bathroom. I don't question him. I can't think. The memory of the CB chirping and the sound of static rings in my ears. I see the open door and horror grips my throat hard. I change quickly and think about calling Mel, but I can't. If she's in trouble, it'll make it worse. Maybe she's fine and they just found out that Sean hired hookers. That means that they might be looking for me.

I pull on the modest dress and change my shoes to a ballet flat. There's make-up remover and a pair of glasses. I lighten my eye shadow and lipstick, and then pin back my hair. After I put on the glasses, I look like a vintage Jackie O. I blink at my reflection, heart pounding, and try to look normal.

It feels like everyone is watching me, but no one even glances my way. People are huddled together, talking in quiet tones, saying things that I can't hear. A couple passes me after showing their room key to the guards at the door while others do the same thing at the elevator bank. A man hurries past me and out the front doors. He's wearing a suit with a red tie.

His voice booms as he explains, "There was an unfortunate event here this evening, and we don't want to make it more difficult on the family than it already is. Please separate..." his voice dies as the doors close behind him.

It's not true. It can't be. I don't know what happened in that room and I can't leave this place until I find out. I don't care what Black does to me or if I incriminate myself. I'm frozen in place, halfway between the doors and the elevators when my phone vibrates.

It's Marty. I pick up without thinking and he starts spewing questions at me before I can say anything. "What the hell happened? Are you guys all right? They said on the news that there'd been a violent crime, but they didn't say anything else. Then, Ferro's name popped up and, my God—tell me that you're all right. Tell me that bastard didn't hurt you."

"I'm fine. He didn't hurt me. Sean didn't hurt anyone, but I think something happened to Mel. Gabe is waiting for me outside. He wants to take me back to Black's but I can't leave her here. I can't leave." My voice trails off and I already realize what I'm doing. Walking past the guard, I flash my room key card and step into the elevator, and press the button.

Marty is scolding me, telling me to get the hell out of there, but I don't understand the rest. As soon as I'm standing in the metal box, the connection is lost. I turn off my phone and shove it into my purse, and press the button.

When the doors open I have a strange sense of déjà vu, except last time I was here, I was happy. Glancing down at the ring on my finger, I take a step. I'm out of the elevator and onto the hallway carpet. There's a uniformed police officer with his back to me. Someone inside the room is talking to him. Every step I take feels unreal as I brace myself for whatever I might see. Mel can't be dead, she can't be, but when the open doorway comes into view I freeze.

There's a limp, mocha-colored wrist lying on a blood stained carpet. The manicured fingers are curled and still. Her forearm disappears beneath a white sheet and the black bead from her bracelet is shattered next to her on the carpet. I stand there and stare, unable to move. My mind rejects what my eyes are telling me.

Everything around me floats away as horror slams down hard on my shoulders, making my knees buckle, and forcing me to the floor.

TURN THE PAGE TO READ A FREE
SAMPLE OF:

THE
PROPOSITION
BRYAN FERRO

A Ferro Family serial coming November 2013!

THE PROPOSITION

Vol. 1

The sky is clear except for a few white glittering stars. They're hung high out of reach, impossibly beautiful and distant. The air has that crisp fall scent, and I know there will be frost tonight. Dad would have covered his plants with plastic to get a few more weeks from their fragile lives. The tarp is in the basement, still folded, where he kept it. The pansies will freeze and fade. This is their last night in this house, as it is mine.

Pushing the swing on the back porch with the tip of my foot, I start it swaying again. Life is so fleeting, so meaningless. The hole that's swallowing me is relentless. I thought I'd cry more, but I haven't even been able to do that. The tears won't fall. Neil says it's because my father's death hasn't hit me yet, but it has. The weight of his loss is pressing so hard on my shoulders that I can't lift my face from the dirt. For all those years, it was just the two of us. He was always there for me. He saved me from incomprehensible misery and now that he's gone, I find myself back in the shallows, unable to escape.

My eyes sweep over the wooden fence, taking in the rotten boards. Things were tight and I knew Dad sacrificed for me, I just had no idea how much until now. My college bills, my car, and all the things I needed were paid for without a blink, but I never stopped to wonder where the money came from. Dad worked hard, so I assumed it was enough.

I was wrong.

There hasn't been enough for a long time, and I had no idea. He never said anything. When I came home from classes at the end of the day, he'd hand me a twenty and tell me to be a kid and go have fun. He said stuff like that all the time. It makes me wonder if he knew what was coming, but there's no way he foresaw this.

When I came home from class last week, I found him in the yard, face down in a pile of leaves. My throat tightens and I push away the memory. It's not something that I ever want to see again, but it lights up over and over again. My senses are overloaded. I can still feel Dad's cold skin and the weight of his lifeless body as I rolled him over. The texture of his tattered flannel jacket is still on my fingertips. The sound of my strangled voice crying out his name over and over again still rings in my ears. I never felt so afraid. For the first time in a long time, I am alone.

My phone is on the wooden swing and chirps next to me. I don't feel like talking.

Silence has encased me inside a tomb of misery since that day. Neil stood next to me and held my hand until hours blurred into days. Neil didn't want to leave me alone here tonight, but I insisted. It's my last night in this house. I'll never step over the threshold again. I'll never catch the scent of my father's aftershave in his little bathroom. All the memories will be lost and it will be like he never existed.

~COMING NOVEMBER 2013~

The Story of Bryan Ferro

MORE FERRO FAMILY BOOKS

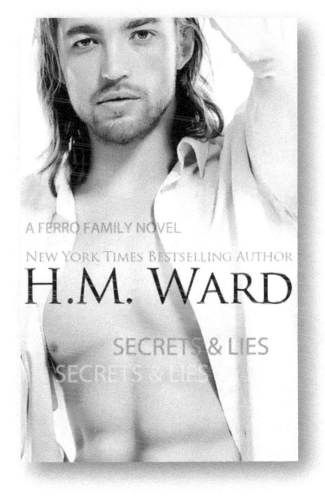

SECRETS & LIES

BRYAN FERRO
~THE PROPOSITION~
Coming in November 2013

*****

SEAN FERRO
~THE ARRANGEMENT~

******

PETER FERRO GRANZ
~DAMAGED~

******

JONATHAN FERRO
~STRIPPED~

MORE ROMANCE BOOKS BY

H.M. WARD

DAMAGED

THE ARRANGEMENT

STRIPPED

SCANDALOUS

SCANDALOUS 2

SECRETS

THE SECRET LIFE OF TRYSTAN
SCOTT

And more.

To see a full book list, please visit:

www.SexyAwesomeBooks.com/books.htm